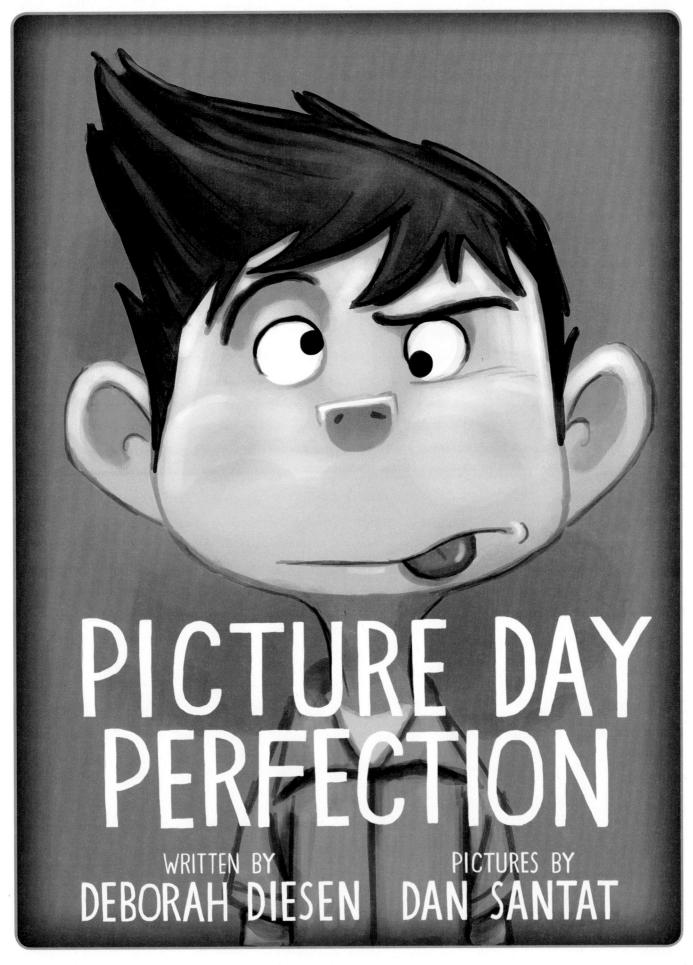

PICTURE DAY PERFECTION

WRITTEN BY
DEBORAH DIESEN

PICTURES BY
DAN SANTAT

SCHOLASTIC INC.

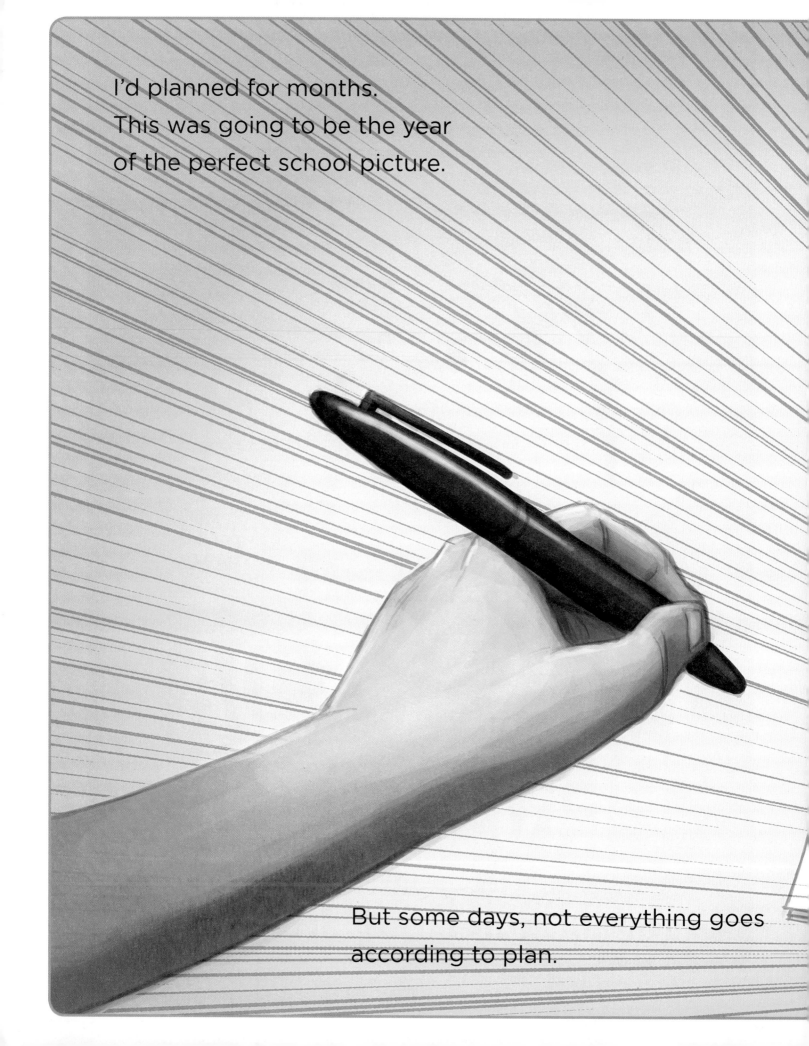

I'd planned for months.
This was going to be the year
of the perfect school picture.

But some days, not everything goes
according to plan.

The day started with the worst case of bedhead *ever*.

Exhibit A: Front view

Exhibit C: Back view

Exhibit B: Side view

Exhibit D: The look on my brother's face when he saw my hair.

Then it took me *quite* some time to unearth my favorite shirt. I finally found it at the *very* bottom of the hamper.

You might call it "stained."
You might call it "wrinkled."
You might even call it "smelly."
You wouldn't be wrong.

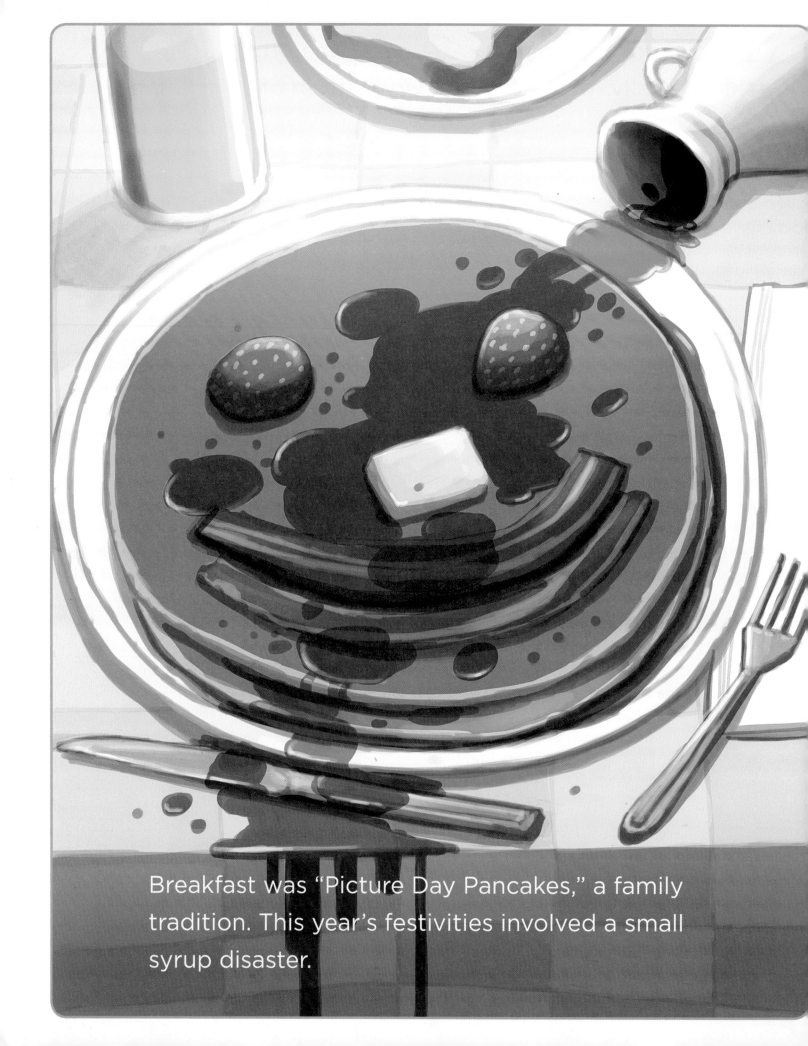

Breakfast was "Picture Day Pancakes," a family tradition. This year's festivities involved a small syrup disaster.

More accurately described as a *large* syrup disaster.
And it occurred exactly as the bus pulled up.

I had a feeling we'd be getting a new family tradition.

On the bus, I got into a small bit of trouble.

Make that a *large* bit of trouble.
The bus driver made me sit in the seat
right behind him for the rest of the ride.

By the time I got into school, my picture
day face was fixed in a *scowl*.

In class, Mrs. Smith collected our photo order forms. Do you think my mom checked "Emerald Green" for my photo background? Or "Peacock Blue?" Or "Pizzazzy Purple"? No. Once again, of all the backgrounds in the world, Mom checked snoring-boring "Traditional Gray."

No one gets "Traditional Gray."

Except for me.

And it just so happens to be the only color in the
world that makes my favorite shirt disappear.
All but the stains and the wrinkles.

After that, the teacher had us all stand up and practice our Picture Day smiles. Personally, I thought we needed a little something to get us in the Picture Day mood.

Whoops!

Got myself in trouble.

Again.

Luckily, I got to rejoin the class in time for Art.
Art involved quite a lot of paint.

Or at least it did for *me*.

Finally, it was time to line up for our photos.

Ned, just in front of me, got the *last* complimentary plastic comb.

I watched as classmate after classmate smiled for the camera. I got queasy listening to everyone say "Cheese."

I can't *stand* cheese.

The mere thought of it turns me green! *Deeply* green. And just as my face reached its most *awful* pea-green shade, it was . . . *my turn.*

I stepped forward.

I sat down on the stool.

It was hard as a rock, and cold as an iceberg.

"Just a sec," said the photographer as he fiddled with the camera knobs.

As I sat and waited, everything that had happened rushed through my mind. The monstrous messes. The muddles and the mix-ups. The whole day, from the moment I'd rolled out of bed, had gone . . .

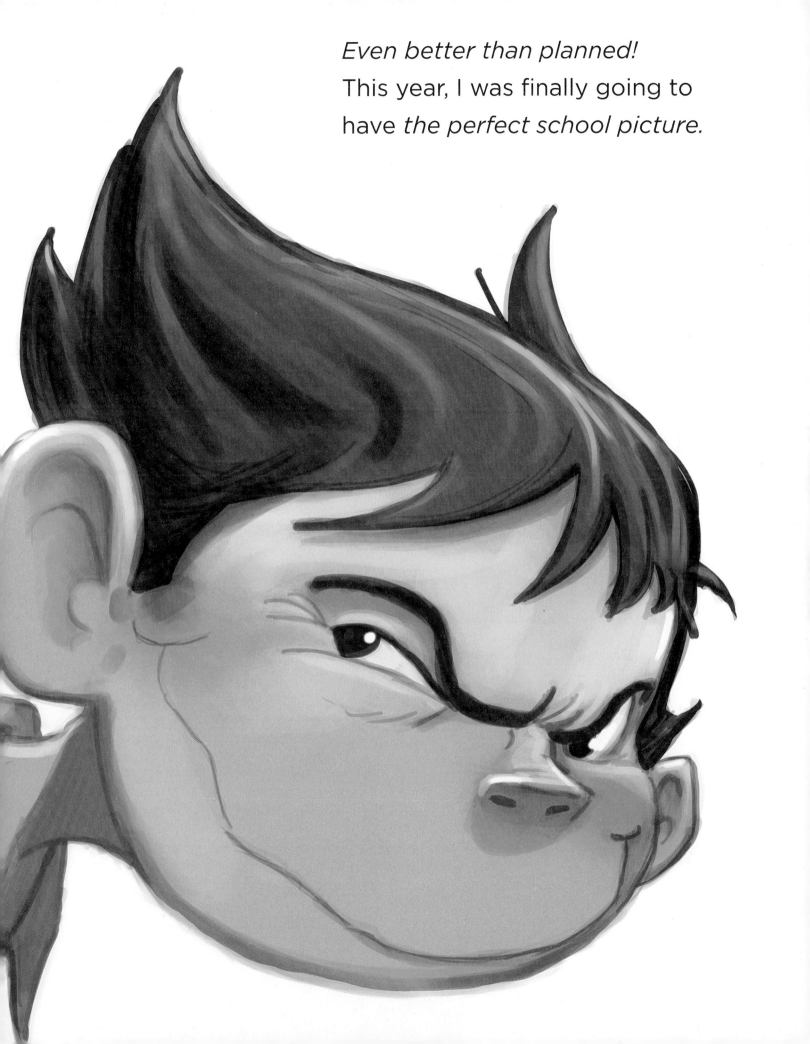

Even better than planned!
This year, I was finally going to
have *the perfect school picture.*

And that's when I heard a

CLICK

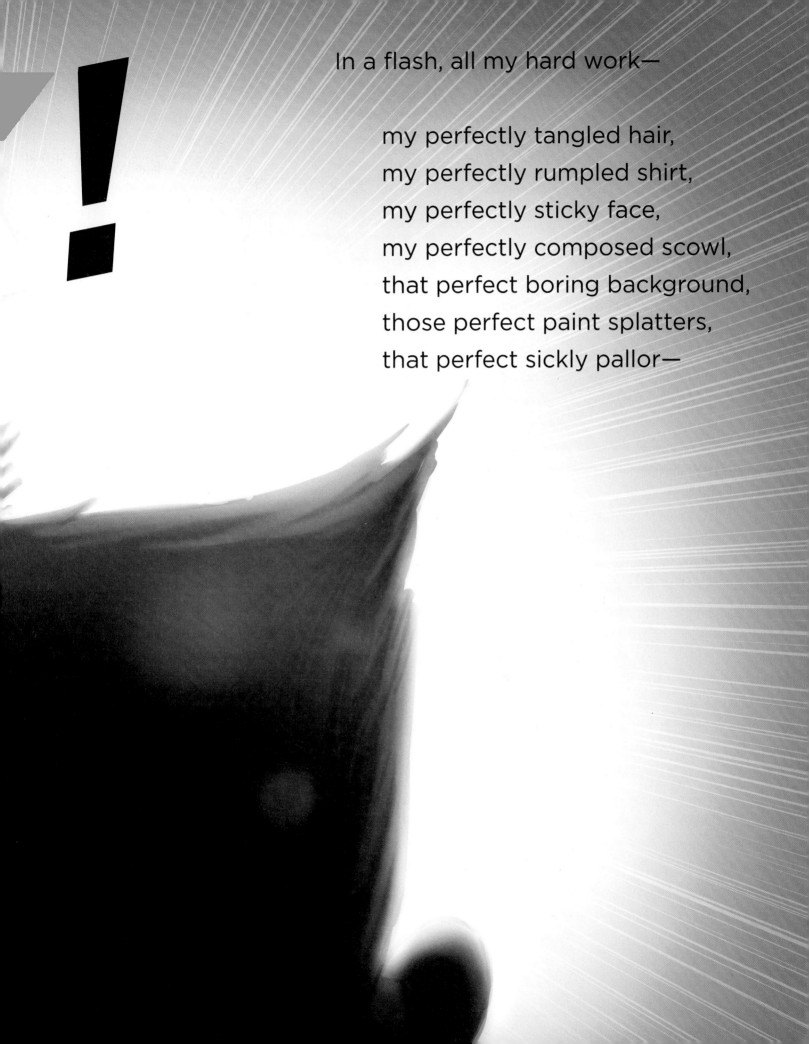

In a flash, all my hard work—

my perfectly tangled hair,
my perfectly rumpled shirt,
my perfectly sticky face,
my perfectly composed scowl,
that perfect boring background,
those perfect paint splatters,
that perfect sickly pallor—

WASTED!
USELESS!
RUINED,

in a moment of weakness,
by an unexpected smile.

Mom says it's my best picture ever.

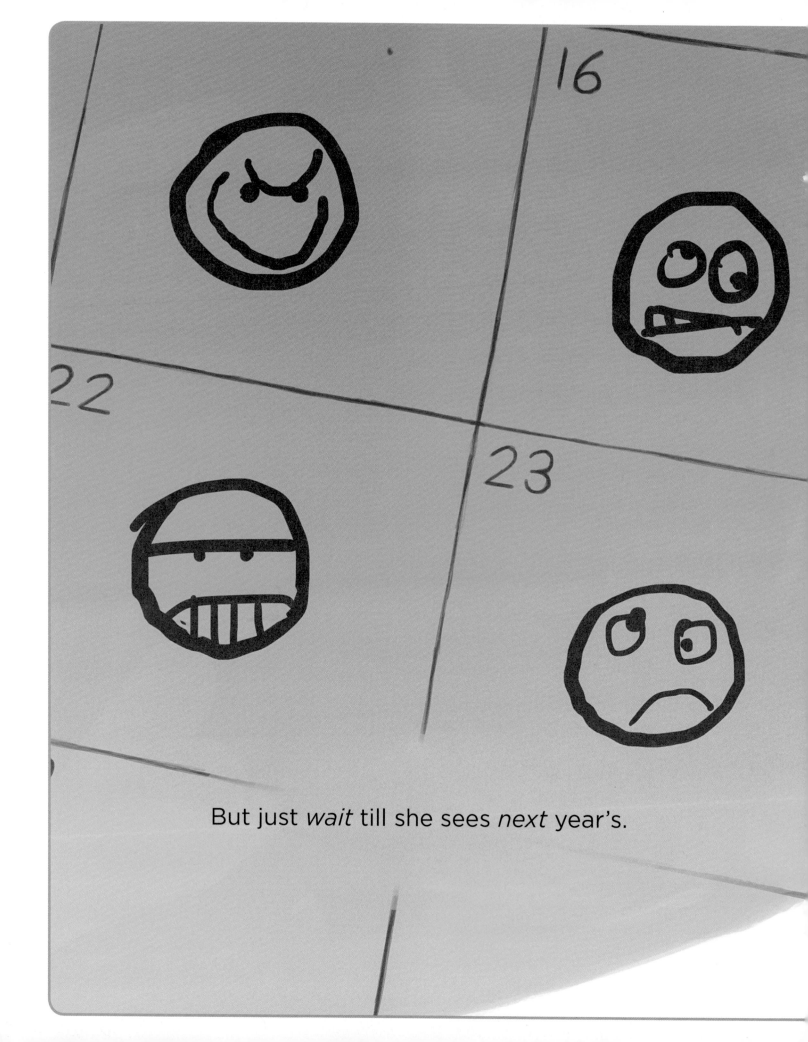

But just *wait* till she sees *next* year's.

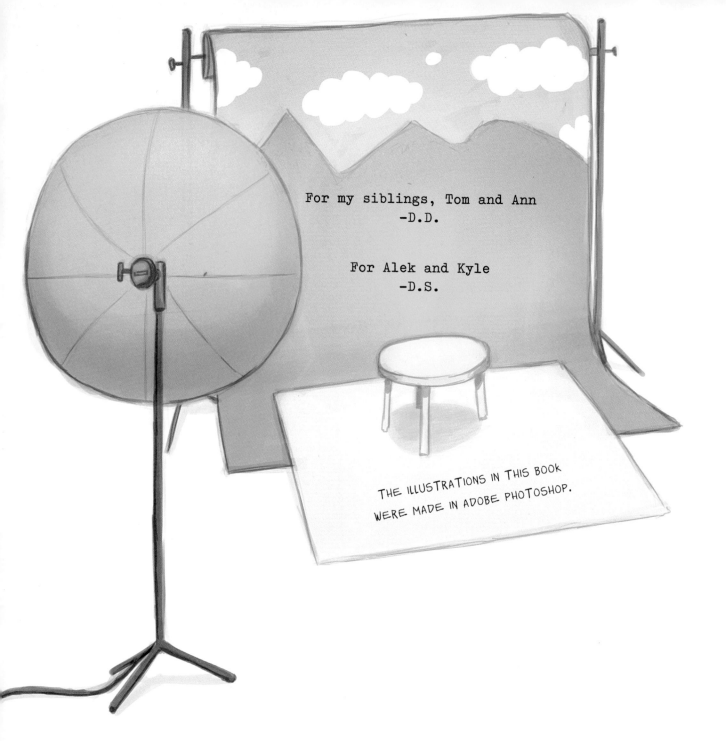

For my siblings, Tom and Ann
-D.D.

For Alek and Kyle
-D.S.

THE ILLUSTRATIONS IN THIS BOOK
WERE MADE IN ADOBE PHOTOSHOP.

ISBN 978-0-545-80227-7

Text copyright © 2013 by Deborah Diesen. Illustrations copyright © 2013 by Dan Santat. All rights reserved. Published by Scholastic Inc., 557 Broadway, New York, NY 10012, by arrangement with Abrams Books for Young Readers, an imprint of Harry N. Abrams, Inc. SCHOLASTIC and associated logos are trademarks and/or registered trademarks of Scholastic Inc.

12 11 10 9 8 7 6 5 4 3 2   14 15 16 17 18 19/0

Printed in the U.S.A.   40

First Scholastic printing, September 2014

Book design by Chad W. Beckerman